Seeing Sky ★ Blue Pink

Seeing Sky ★ Blue Pink

CANDICE RANSOM

 CAROLRHODA BOOKS, INC. MINNEAPOLIS • NEW YORK

Carolrhoda Books, Inc.
A division of Lerner Publishing Group, Inc.
241 First Avenue North
Minneapolis, MN 55401 U.S.A.

Website address: www.lernerbooks.com

Library of Congress Cataloging-in-Publication Data

Ransom, Candice F., 1952–
    Seeing sky-blue pink / by Candice Ransom.
        p.   cm.
    Summary: Although fearful at first, eight-year-old Maddie soon begins to
enjoy living in the country and getting to know her new stepfather.
    ISBN: 978-0-8225-7142-1 (lib. bdg. : alk. paper)
    [1. Stepfathers—Fiction. 2. Remarriage—Fiction. 3. Moving,
Household—Fiction. 4. Fear—Fiction. 5. Country life—Fiction.] I. Title.
PZ7.R1743Se 2007
[Fic]—dc22   2006101326

Manufactured in the United States of America
1 2 3 4 5 6 – BP – 12 11 10 09 08 07

To My Sister Patricia

Contents

Asking the Cat

"How about a wheelbarrow ride?" Sam asked. He tamped the earth around the base of the dogwood tree he had just planted.

Maddie looked doubtfully at the dirty wheelbarrow. Is that the way people got around in the country? In Manassas, she and her mother took the bus.

"Where to?" she asked.

"Mrs. Tompkins' house, just down the road," Sam said. "She wants to meet you."

The window in Maddie's bedroom screeched up. Her mother poked her head out. "Sam, the tree is beautiful. Maddie, did you know Sam dug that wild tree from the woods?"

"Mom, I'm riding in the wheelbarrow to Mrs. Tompkins'!"

"Oh, Maddie, I'm afraid it will rain."

Maddie hoped her mother wouldn't say no. "I don't care if I get wet."

Her mother glanced at Sam. "Doesn't it look like rain?"

"Let's ask Abraham. He'll know." Sam bent down to the big black cat that lay stretched in the grass.

Maddie laughed. "Ask a *cat* the weather!"

Abraham sat up and glared at Maddie with slitted eyes. She stopped laughing.

"Cats know more than people give them credit for," Sam said.

"How do they tell us?"

"They have ways." In a loud voice, Sam said, "Abraham, will it rain this afternoon?"

The cat yawned, then scratched behind his left ear.

"Sunny!" Sam declared.

Maddie's mother laughed. "If Abraham says so. Have fun, you two."

"What if it was going to rain?" Maddie asked Sam. "What would Abraham do?"

"Scratch his right ear," Sam replied.

Maddie looked at the cat with new respect. "I wish Abraham would sleep on my bed. But he doesn't even come when I call him. He doesn't like me."

"He doesn't know you yet. Give him time."

Before they married Sam, Maddie and her mother used to have Perfect Days. On Perfect Days, Maddie shared a maple walnut sundae at Rudy's, visited the library, and rubbed the left hoof of the horse statue in the park, for luck.

Now Maddie had a new father, her own bedroom in a real house, and a cat that could tell the weather. It was a lot to get used to all at once. She wondered if she would have Perfect Days in the country.

Sam tipped the wheelbarrow and brushed out the loose dirt. "Ready?"

"Can Buckingham come too?" Maddie never went anywhere without her stuffed donkey. Patches of gray fur had been worn away. Buckingham's legs hung like old socks. One arm dangled from a few threads.

Maddie worried that Sam would laugh at her about Buckingham, like the kids at school did. "Sissy-baby," they called her.

But Sam said, "Buckingham would probably like a change of scenery." He steadied the wheelbarrow so Maddie could climb in.

"Am I too big?" she asked.

"You're just the right size."

Maddie crawled into the wheelbarrow. "Mom says I'm small for eight. And my feet *never* grow. Other kids make fun of my feet."

"You just don't have as much turned up on the ground," said Sam.

Was that supposed to be funny? Should she laugh? Maddie bit her lip. She wished she knew what to say.

"Here we go." Sam lifted the handles and rolled the wheelbarrow across the yard.

Maddie tucked Buckingham between her knees. She gripped the sides of the wheelbarrow as she bumped down their driveway and onto the side of the road. The fat front tire bounced over gravel. It was hard keeping her rear end from bouncing, too.

"Okay?" Sam called.

"Ye-es-es-es!" Her voice juddered over each stone.

They rolled past two houses and a barn. A pony with a shaggy mane stared at them. Maddie wanted to wave, but couldn't let go.

Sam turned at a battered mailbox. A white clapboard house sat on a tiny lawn. Ruffly pink flowers bloomed along the fence. A battered pickup truck hunkered in front of an old garage.

Sam stopped the wheelbarrow by the back porch. Several red hens flustered around, chuckling at their arrival.

A woman wearing an apron over men's pants stepped out of the house. She drew a handful of corn from her apron pocket and scattered the kernels in a wide arc. The hens waddled over to gobble their lunch.

"You must be Maddie," the woman said, smiling. "I'm Eliza Tompkins."

"Hi." Maddie climbed out of the wheelbarrow with Buckingham.

"Sam, why haven't you brought this child over sooner?"

"Sorry, Miss Eliza," he replied. "Between the garden and my orders and moving Maddie and Sharon's things into the house—"

"You could have come by for ten minutes," she chided. "Well, you're here now, Maddie. Come inside."

Maddie followed Mrs. Tompkins into the kitchen. It smelled like wet wool and woodsmoke, even though it was late summer. She looked around. A heavy wooden rocking chair draped with sweaters was pulled up to the stove. A leather Bible, bristling with bookmarks, rested on the table. Plants with purple flowers and fuzzy green leaves lined the windowsill.

Maddie liked this room. In their apartment in town, the kitchen was dark, with ugly yellow walls that stayed greasy no matter how hard her mother scrubbed them. Maddie touched one of the plants' fuzzy leaves. It was soft as a kitten's ear.

Sam came in and hung the red ballcap he always wore on a nail by the door. "I unloaded that sack of feed from your truck and put it in the chicken house."

"You're an angel." Mrs. Tompkins set a meringue-covered pie on the table. "I dropped a fork this morning, so I baked a pie."

"What?" asked Maddie.

Sam grinned at her as they sat down. "There's an old saying, 'Fork falls, lady calls.' Miss Eliza means she knew a lady was coming to visit."

"Oh." She was worried about the kind of filling

under the blanket of meringue. What if it was lemon? She hated lemon.

"Butterscotch?" Sam asked Mrs. Tompkins.

"What else? Butterscotch is Sam's favorite." Mrs. Tompkins' knife sliced through a cloud of meringue. Underneath lay soft, brownish-yellow custard. She gave the first piece to Maddie.

"I've never had this kind before," said Maddie, taking the smallest bite possible. With her tongue, she smooshed the meringue against the roof of her mouth. It was good!

"How do you like living in the country, Maddie?" asked Mrs. Tompkins.

"I've only been here a week," Maddie said. She wasn't sure she liked living in the country, but didn't want to say so.

She did miss drawing with chalk on the sidewalk in front of their apartment building. And riding her bike. But there were no sidewalks in the country. And she couldn't ride her bike on the busy highway.

Mrs. Tompkins nodded at Buckingham, who was sitting quietly in Maddie's lap. "We haven't been properly introduced."

"This is Buckingham. I've had her since I was four." Maddie didn't say her father had given her the small donkey the morning he left Maddie and her mother.

"Her?" asked Mrs. Tompkins. "Isn't Buckingham a boy's name?"

"*My* Buckingham is a girl," Maddie said patiently. She always had to explain about Buckingham's name.

Mrs. Tompkins took Buckingham's paw, the one that was loose, and shook it gently. "Pleased to meet you." To Sam, she asked, "How's your garden doing?"

"I need to plow that last acre," he replied. "I saw that flat of cabbage plants by your shed. Better get them in the ground soon."

"Is it going to rain?" asked Mrs. Tompkins.

"Abraham says it will be sunny," Maddie said.

"That cat is never wrong," said Sam.

"Maddie," said Mrs. Tompkins. "I notice you came in the wheelbarrow taxi. Can you carry a piece of pie and an African violet for your mother?"

"Is that what those fuzzy plants are called?" Maddie asked.

"I've been raising African violets for forty years." Mrs. Tompkins went over to the windowsill. "Which one do you think your mother would like?"

Maddie considered the row of pots. Some were deep purple, some a lighter shade. Some had single blossoms, while others grew clusters of blossoms.

"That one." She pointed to a plant with light purple blooms.

"Good choice." Mrs. Tompkins ripped a paper sack in half. Then she set the pot into it. "Now you won't get dirt all over."

"Need me to do anything else before we go, Miss Eliza?" Sam asked.

"Thanks, Sam. Can't think of a thing right this minute."

Maddie lingered in the doorway. "Is this a farm?"

"Used to be," Mrs. Tompkins said. "Back when my husband was alive. We kept cows and goats and raised a truck garden. We were never blessed with children, but I had nearly a hundred laying hens. I still keep a few around for company."

"After Mr. Tompkins passed," Sam said, "Miss Eliza didn't need such a big place, so she sold most of the land. I bought five acres after I came home from the navy. She saved the prettiest parcel for me."

Maddie watched Mrs. Tompkins cut a large wedge of pie and wrap it in a see-through square of paper. Mrs. Tompkins handed the bundle to Maddie.

"This stuff is weird," Maddie said, touching the smooth paper. It felt like an almost used-up white crayon.

"It's wax paper," said Sam. "In the fall, we'll find leaves and make wax paper pictures. We'd better skedaddle. Your mother will think we joined the circus."

Mrs. Tompkins followed them outside. Tipping her head back, she studied the sky. "I still think it wants to rain."

"Here come your chickens," Maddie said.

"Did I call you?" Mrs. Tompkins asked them, her fists on her hips.

Unconcerned, the chickens eddied around her feet, hoping for more corn.

"Your chickens have names?" said Maddie.

"Of course. Chickens are all different, just like people." Mrs. Tompkins counted the milling red heads. "Somebody's missing. Maisie . . . Sadie . . . Lula . . . *Gert*!"

"Gert's always fooling around," said Sam.

"Gert!" Mrs. Tompkins called. "Gertie Tompkins! Get over here!"

A chicken flew out from under a bush, yellow legs flying.

Mrs. Tompkins sighed. "Miss High-and-Mighty has a mind of her own."

Maddie was amazed. In the country, animals came when they were called! Though Abraham didn't come when she called him.

"Let's shove off, Maddie," Sam said.

"Thanks for the pie," Maddie said to Mrs. Tompkins.

"Tell your mama to come by. And don't you be a stranger neither."

How she could be a stranger after they'd met and even eaten pie together? Maddie scrambled into the wheelbarrow and held Buckingham between her knees. Sam put the plant and pie along one side.

The ride home seemed shorter, the way it always did when you had already been someplace.

"Look how fast we got here," she told Sam.

"It may seem fast to you, but not to me," he said, puffing up their driveway. "Going home it's uphill."

Maddie thought about her afternoon. The wheel-

barrow taxi. Butterscotch pie. Wax paper. Meeting a
chicken with a mind of its own. She never did those
things in town.

Sam rolled the wheelbarrow into the shed.

They walked across the yard to the dogwood tree
outside Maddie's window. Their shadows were caught
in the branches of the tree's shadow.

Taller trees grew beyond Sam's workshop and the
garden. The woods. Maddie's looked back at her dogwood. "How did you roll the wheelbarrow through
the woods?" she asked.

"I couldn't," said Sam. "I carried the tree on my
back."

A whole tree! That must have been heavy, Maddie thought.

"My tree doesn't look so good," she said. The leaves
hung loose, like Buckingham's arm.

"It just needs to get used to living here," Sam said.
"Once it sets roots, it'll be fine. You'll like this tree. It
has white flowers in the spring. And red leaves in the
fall with little red berries."

Abraham ambled over. Maddie wondered if the cat answered other questions besides the weather. Sam said his cat knew everything. Would Abraham know if she was going to like having a father again? Could he tell her if she would have Perfect Days in the country?

The cat sat on his haunches and scratched briskly under his chin.

"Look!" Maddie said. "Abraham is scratching in a new place. What does that mean?"

"Probably means change is in the air," Sam said.

Maddie still wasn't sure she could believe a cat.

"Maybe," she said, "Abraham has fleas."

Sky ★ Blue Pink

"Sam, would you pick up some paint chips at the store today?" Maddie's mother said one morning. "We're painting your room this weekend, Maddie. What color would you like?"

"I don't know." Maddie had never picked out paint colors before. She'd never had a bedroom, either. In the apartment, she slept in the living room on a fold-out sofa.

Sam was writing out the bill for an oak cabinet he had finished the day before. He made furniture in his workshop.

"How about sky-blue pink?" he said to Maddie, re-checking his numbers.

"That's not a real color."

"It *is* a real color. Haven't you ever seen sky-blue pink?"

Maddie gave him a suspicious look. She still couldn't tell when Sam was teasing her. "Is this another one of those trick questions?"

He laughed. "You mean, like who is buried in Grant's tomb? What color is George Washington's white horse?"

Maddie couldn't believe she had been fooled by those silly riddles. A *baby* could have figured them out.

"Ready to work in the garden with me?" he asked.

"Let me get my shoes." She ran down the hall and into her bedroom.

Maddie loved her room. One window faced mountains Sam said were the Blue Ridge. She could make out gentle bluish hills through the branches of her dogwood tree. Sam watered her tree every night, and now the leaves were green and bright.

Her bed was tucked under the other window. If Maddie crawled to the foot, she could see Sam's workshop, the garden, and the woods lurking beyond.

At night Maddie pulled her shade to the windowsill. That's what she did at the apartment.

After her father went away, Maddie and Buckingham waited for him every day by the window. Maddie stared down at the street, but her father's car never rounded the corner.

Then her parents got a divorce. Maddie drew the shades near her fold-out sofa to keep out leaping shadows.

Here, the black trees reminded her of goblins. She wondered if the trees crept forward in the dark. If snakes and bears hid behind their trunks.

Buckingham leaned against Maddie's pillow.

"C'mon, Bucky. Let's go to the garden." She grabbed Buckingham, her tennis shoes, and raced back to the kitchen.

Maddie's mother was packing a lunch.

"Two sandwiches, peanut-butter crackers, brownies, and oranges," said Maddie's mother, putting napkins in Sam's gray metal lunch box. "Plus a thermos of sweet tea. That should hold you two." She clamped the thermos into the humped lid.

Maddie admired Sam's grown-up lunch box. Kid lunch boxes with cartoon characters on them seemed dumb to her. But this! This was a lunch box worth carrying.

Sam scooped the lunchbox off the counter. His arm swung down as if he'd just picked up a great weight.

"We're only going to plow that back acre, not half the county," he said.

Maddie's mother gave them a playful shove toward the door. "Maddie, be careful on that tractor."

Maddie ran out into the morning sunshine. A mockingbird fussed at them from the clothesline as they walked past Sam's workshop to the tractor shed.

Sam set the lunch box in the shade of the persimmon tree, then unlocked the door. A red and gray tractor dozed in the cobwebby gloom.

"What an old tractor," Maddie remarked. "It should be in a museum!"

"Lots of people would give their eyeteeth to own old Gray Goose."

"Who?" She didn't see any goose, old or young.

Sam slapped the tractor hood. "My Ford Ferguson. They don't make 'em like this anymore."

Everything, it seemed, had a name at Sam's house. Even his pickup truck was named Chester.

"Hop up," he said.

Maddie hesitated. She was to short to reach the step. And she wasn't a good jumper.

"The running board is kind of high." Sam lifted Maddie and Buckingham with his two hands, swinging her up onto the step.

"There's no place for me to sit," she said.

"Hang on to the fender," Sam said. "The best view is behind, anyway." He hoisted himself into the driver's seat and turned the ignition key.

The Gray Goose coughed twice, then sputtered to life. The tractor chugged out of the shed, across the yard, and into the patch that Sam had already cleared of bushes and weeds. He pulled a lever and lowered the plow.

Gripping the fender, Maddie watched the plow bite into ground. Waves of red earth parted on either side of the blade.

She was afraid she would get sick riding backward, but she didn't. She was too busy noticing things that churned to the surface. Rocks, worms, rusty bottle caps.

The Gray Goose plowed in circles that became smaller and smaller. The sun climbed into the sky. It grew hot.

At last Sam switched off the engine. They hopped off the tractor and walked over to the persimmon tree. They sat down in the shade. Maddie put Buckingham on grass as soft as a clean towel.

Sam opened the lunch box and handed Maddie the

thermos. She carefully poured two cups of chilled tea.

"Your mother is a good cook," he said, unwrapping a pimento cheese sandwich. He ate faster than anybody Maddie had ever seen. His sandwich disappeared in three bites.

She nibbled a peanut-butter cracker, then got up and squatted at the edge of the garden. With a stick, she dug into the freshly turned dirt.

A fat, pink worm wriggled around her stick. Gently she let him go. Then her stick unearthed a flat, white rock, pointed on one end. The edges were chipped.

"Look what I found." Maddie showed the rock to Sam.

He held it between his thumb and forefinger. "An arrowhead! Don't see many of these anymore."

"Indians lived here?" She had learned about Native Americans in school.

He nodded. "A long time ago. But they left when settlers—people like us who came from other countries—came to live here."

"Where did the Indians go?"

"West, mostly," he replied. "Later some of the set-tlers went west too. But somebody has always lived on this land. They left things behind to tell us they were here."

Maddie put the arrowhead in her pocket. "What will we leave for other people to find?"

"One thing I don't want to leave is a mess." Sam stuffed their trash in the lunchbox. "I have to get those paint chips for your mother. Want to go to George's?"

"Yes!"

They walked back to the garage and got into Chester, Sam's old green pickup. They drove a short distance down the highway, then pulled into a parking lot in front of a small brick building.

Maddie had been to George's only one other time, but she adored the little store. It smelled like sawdust and fresh bologna. Boxes of boots towered over kerosene lanterns. Purple pickled eggs bobbed in a big jar. Loaves of squishy white bread, the kind

Maddie's mother never bought, were piled next to bags of pork rinds.

"How are you today?" George asked as they entered.

"Fine," Maddie answered. The storekeeper spoke English, but with an accent. She wondered if he was one of the people Sam had talked about.

"Are you a settler?" she asked.

George and Sam both laughed.

"I came here from Greece twenty-three years ago," said George. "So, yes, I guess you could say I'm a settler."

"I'm one, too," Maddie said. "I've only been here a week. Before, I lived in Manassas."

"The town is nice," said George. "But the country is better. You will like it here."

"I can't draw with my chalk because we don't have a sidewalk," she said. "Or ride my bike. Or have a maple walnut sundae at Rudy's."

"You'll find other things to do," George told her. "Go camping. Or build a tree house."

Maddie stared at him. Go camping! Build a tree house! In those wild woods?

"Let's go pick out paint chips, kiddo," Sam said.

Maddie worried Sam might be mad at her. She should have told George she loved the country. Even if she wasn't sure she did.

On one of the crowded aisles was a stand displaying paper strips with bands of colors. They didn't look like the chips Maddie had pictured. She thought they would be like chocolate chips, only in rainbow colors.

"I like pink," Maddie said, taking strips with shades of pink. "Baby Pink, Fairy Tale Pink. I never knew there were so many kinds of pink."

"Hmmm. I don't see sky-blue pink," Sam said.

"There is no sky-blue pink!" Maddie was indignant. "That color doesn't even make sense. How can blue sky be pink?"

"Guess I'll have to prove it to you."

Then Maddie spotted something above the paint cans. Lunch boxes just like Sam's! Some were gray and some were black, but they all had the same humped shape.

He saw her looking at them. "Would you like one of those?"

"Yes! I can carry my things in it."

"Then I'll get one for you."

"Thanks!" Maddie waited for him to pull a gray one off the shelf.

Instead he inspected a black lunch box for dents. "This one's good."

Maddie was disappointed. She really wanted a gray one. But maybe Sam didn't want her to have one exactly like his.

They walked up front. Sam set the lunch box on the counter and Maddie added the paint chips.

"Paint chips free," said George. "And for today, so is this. It's not a maple walnut sundae from Rudy's, but my grandkids love 'em." He took a Dixie cup from the ice cream freezer and gave it to Maddie with a flourish.

"Thanks a lot!"

Maddie pulled off the lid and licked it clean. Then she unwrapped the flat wooden spoon that reminded her of the "ahh" sticks her doctor used. She scooped sweet ice cream, scraping equal amounts of vanilla and chocolate so each bite tasted perfect.

They drove home. Sam went to his workshop to finish sanding a TV stand. Maddie went in the house to her room.

She put the arrowhead and her sidewalk chalk in her new lunch box. The dull black metal reminded her of a blackboard. Taking a piece of blue chalk, she printed her name on the side.

Then, with the heel of her hand, she rubbed it off. She didn't want Sam to think she couldn't take care of the things he got her.

But she could still make out a faint *MADDIE*. Like the people who lived here before, a trace of herself remained.

Maddie and Buckingham sat on the back porch steps.

Abraham lay at one end, licking his stomach vigorously, as if he'd worked in a coal mine all day.

The paint chips were fanned out around Maddie. She couldn't decide between Watermelon Pink and Spring Tulip.

Through the kitchen door she heard the rhythmic *clink-clink* as her mother dried each piece of silverware and dropped it into the drawer. At supper her mother had asked Maddie to choose a color, since they were going to buy the paint tomorrow.

Sam came out carrying a plastic bag of trash. He scanned the sky. "Guess what? Your favorite color is about to appear."

"What color?" Maddie glanced up. The sun was sliding behind the woods.

He sat down beside her. "Sky-blue pink, what else?"

Maddie pursed her lips. "That color is not on any of my chalks or crayons. Or these paint papers. It's not real."

"This color is better than any color you've ever seen.

I promise. Just watch."

Puffy sheep clouds floated across the blue-sky field. The orange sun ball seemed stuck on top of the trees, with just a slice showing, like Abraham's tongue.

Then, as if a magician waved his wand, the puffy white clouds became tinted the softest pink. Hints of blue sky filtered through, creating a new color, blue and pink together.

"Sky-blue pink," Maddie breathed. "So *that's* what it looks like."

"The best part is coming."

The sun edged below the horizon, striking the clouds with shafts of orange. Electrified pink streaks arrowed across the sky. Blue still showed through, but the pink was so strong, Maddie half expected the clouds to speak.

They would sound like God, she thought.

She had never seen color like this before. If a Perfect Day had a color, this would be it. She held up all her paint chips, but the beautiful shade was not on any of them.

"That's the color I want my room," she said. "Can we make it?"

"Only if you remember it," he said. "Can you keep that color in your mind?"

Maddie closed her eyes. Yes! It was there, somehow painted on the back of her eyelids.

She opened her eyes. Closed them again. The beautiful color was still there. She held the color in her mind the way Sam's two hands had lifted her up on the Gray Goose.

She would not lose it.

Fooled at the Dump

After church one Sunday, Sam announced he was going to clean out the basement.

"Thank heavens," said Maddie's mother. "That basement's a sight."

"Can I help?" Maddie asked.

"It's definitely a two-person job," said Sam.

"Change out of your good clothes first," her mother said. "Both of you. Maddie, did you make your bed like I asked you?"

"Um. I sort of forgot."

A tiny line appeared between her mother's eyes. That meant she was serious. "You didn't listen this morning, young lady."

"I'll do it now." In her bedroom, Maddie jerked the covers up, scattering crayons, books, and barrettes. Then she changed into shorts and a T-shirt, and thudded back through the house.

"Boy, what a mess," she said when she and Sam descended the basement stairs. "Looks a whole lot worse than my room."

"I guess I let it get out of hand," he admitted, prodding a dented oilcan with his toe.

Maddie looked down at his feet. "You forgot to change your good shoes."

"So I did. They'll be okay," said Sam. He rubbed his hands together in anticipation of a good afternoon's work. "Let's get busy."

First they cleared the shelves along the cinder block walls. They carried bushel baskets of old cans, jars, broken tools, and scraps of lumber out to Chester.

"What about these old books?" Maddie said, yanking the flaps back on a musty carton. She crinkled her nose at the smell. "Throw them away too?"

"Oh, no. Those books belonged to my grandfather. Should be some storybooks in with his encyclopedias."

Maddie pulled out a dusty volume of *Grimm's Fairy Tales*. She opened the age-mottled covers. Ancient moth-millers fluttered from the yellowed pages like dried rose petals. She put the book on top of the carton. Maybe she'd read it sometime.

Meanwhile Sam had filled two plastic bags with empty coffee cans. "I guess I'm a packrat," he said as they took the bags to the truck, too.

"What are you going to do with all this stuff?" Maddie asked Sam.

"Haul it to the dump."

"What's that?"

Sam slammed Chester's tailgate. "It's where people take their trash."

"At the apartment, the garbage man took our trash," Maddie said.

"Here in the country, we have to get rid of our trash ourselves," said Sam. "I go to the dump at least once a week."

"Can I come, too?"

"Sure, but first I have to wash the basement floor."

Back in the basement, Sam sloshed a bucket of water across the cement floor. Swishing his mop, he chased water and dirt into the drain.

Maddie sat on the stairs with Buckingham and her lunch box. The wall came halfway down the steps, then stopped. She ran her hand over the white plaster. It felt cool and smooth, like the blackboard at school. But this wall was better than a blackboard.

She opened her lunch box and took out a stick of black chalk. The drawing of Abraham the answer cat appeared before she knew what her fingers were up to.

"Pretty good," Sam said, looking up from his mopping. "That's Abraham down to the last whisker."

"I'll clean it off," Maddie said hastily.

"Leave it. It's nice," said Sam. "The basement can use some decorations. Take the whole wall."

"No kidding?" She couldn't believe he was giving her a whole wall just for drawing on!

"Honest and true," he said, squeezing the mop over the bucket. "Ready?"

"Yeah!" Grabbing Buckingham and her lunch box, Maddie raced Sam to the pickup truck.

"No point in running." Sam fastened Maddie's seat belt so Buckingham was protected, too. "Work will always wait."

Maddie wasn't interested in work. She was eager to see the dump.

When Sam turned into the road leading to the dump, Maddie expected mountains of banana peels, soda bottles, and apple cores. Instead she saw big metal bins marked "Phone Books," "Glass," "Cans," and "Plastic."

"What's so exciting about this?" she asked.

"Best part's in the back." Sam drove past the bins and up a bumpy hill. "Know what this hill is made of?"

That was easy. "Dirt."

"Dirt over *garbage*."

"Ewwww!" Maddie held her nose. It *did* stink.

"The fancy name for the dump is the landfill," said Sam. "Every day a bulldozer covers up the trash with more dirt. The landfill keeps getting higher and higher. Soon it'll be the highest spot in the county."

He parked Chester and got out.

Maddie got out, too. A sea of trash stretched before her.

"Don't wander off," Sam warned Maddie. "People aren't careful about what they throw away. You might step on a board with nails sticking up. Or broken glass. Wait for me."

When he had unloaded the truck, Sam said, "Put your feet where I put mine."

"Where are we going?" Maddie asked as they picked their way among boxes and bags.

"Treasure hunting." He nodded toward a teetery

pile of furniture. "Looks like a nice chair somebody got rid of."

By the time they reached the spot, Sam discovered it wasn't such a good chair after all.

"You'd get a big surprise." He poked his hand through the seatless bottom.

"You could cover it with a cloth and when the person sat down, they'd fall right through!" Maddie laughed at her own cleverness.

"Just don't play that joke on me!" But he laughed, too.

"Did you ever find anything good here?" she asked.

"You know that little blue table in the den? Found it here and painted it. Makes a nice planter," he said proudly. "Another time I got a perfectly good fertilizer spreader."

Fertilizer spreaders weren't very interesting. Maddie thought about what she'd like to find at the dump. A *real* treasure, not chairs or plant stands.

She remembered Mrs. Reedy, the landlady at their apartment who wore a ruby ring with diamonds around it. Whenever Mrs. Reedy collected the rent, Maddie always admired her ring. Wouldn't it be something if a rich lady like Mrs. Reedy threw away a box with a real ruby ring in it?

They explored little alleys between heaps of trash. Once Sam thought he had unearthed an antique coffee pot, but it turned out to be an old bleach bottle.

"The dump can fool you," he said, shaking his head over his "discovery." "Makes you think trash is treasure."

But maybe treasure *could* be in the dump, Maddie thought. If she wished hard enough.

Then the sun split the puffy clouds, aiming a beam at a clump of newspapers in the distance. A flash of red glinted like—like a jewel! Maddie drew in her breath and clutched Sam's sleeve.

"Sam!" she cried. "I think I see a ruby ring!"

"What? Are you sure?"

"Yeah!" She pointed. "Over there. I saw something shiny and red. I bet it's a big ruby!"

"I've heard about people finding diamond engagement rings lying right on top of the trash," he said, catching her excitement. "I've never been that lucky, but there's always a first time."

He waded through mounds of grass clippings, an icky cushion, a yellow raincoat, a baby doll minus its head, and a bowed screen door. He stopped to look back at Maddie.

"Am I getting closer?"

"You're warmer," she said.

He maneuvered around a cracked bathtub.

"Warmer!" Maddie said. "Hot! Hot!"

"Where?"

"Past the bicycle handlebars," she directed. "In those newspapers."

Sam stepped on the newspapers, and then his right foot suddenly disappeared.

"Whoa!" Stumbling backward, he pulled his foot out. His shoe was coated in white paint! "Who would leave an open can of paint with newspaper over it?"

Fooled at the Dump

Maddie clapped her hand over her mouth. Was it her fault? If she hadn't wished for a ruby ring, Sam wouldn't have gotten his good shoe covered in paint.

Sam reached down into the newspapers and picked up an object. Clods of wet newspaper fell away in sodden clumps.

"Here's your ruby ring!" he said, holding it up for Maddie to see.

A shiny red metal swing trailed a length of rusted chain.

"How could a swing look like a ring?" she asked.

He worked his way back to her, carrying the swing. "The dump played a trick on you, just like it did me!"

Was he mad at her? She looked at his face. Then she started to laugh. Sam looked so funny with one white shoe and paint spattered halfway up his pant leg!

He hitched up his sock to reveal a painted sock. "What am I going to tell your mother?"

"Tell her you were attacked by a wild paint can!" Maddie laughed so hard she could barely stand.

They walked back to the truck, Sam leaving white footprints like a ghost's tracks.

"Good thing Chester is old," he said, opening the door for Maddie. "I reckon a little paint won't hurt him."

The front seat of Sam's truck was a miniature dump itself, Maddie realized. She brushed aside cellophane cracker wrappers, a steel tape measure, soda straws, and empty coffee cups.

They drove back home, treasure-less.

"I plan to sneak my painted shoe into my shed," Sam said.

But Maddie's mother was in the front yard, plucking dead blooms from the pansies, when they pulled up.

"Uh-oh," said Maddie. She didn't want Sam to get in trouble because of her.

"The dump fooled us," she told her mother quickly.

"That can of paint certainly did," said her mother. "Sam, your jeans and sock aren't worth saving, but I'll try to clean your shoe."

Fooled at the Dump

"We both got in trouble today," Maddie whispered to Sam.

He whispered back, "I think it's okay."

"I heard that." But Maddie's mother was grinning.

After changing into clean clothes, Sam took the swing down into the basement.

Maddie followed him. "What are you going to do?"

"You'll see."

"Swings belong outside," she said.

"Not this kind of swing." He rooted around in a box until he found chains. Removing the rusted chain, he attached the new ones.

"There's no tree down here," Maddie pointed out. "Or swing set. What are you going to hang it from?" She wondered if Sam knew anything about kids at all. Was it harder getting used to a eight-year-old than starting with a baby?

"Oh, ye of little faith." He stood on a stool and looped the chains over the big metal beam that ran the length of the house. "How high do you want it?"

Maddie swallowed. "Not very." She was afraid of high places.

Once, when her father took her to the park, Maddie climbed to the top of the jungle gym. Her father saw her, but could not reach her before she tumbled to the ground. She sprained both her knees.

Sam adjusted the chains until the seat hung low over the basement floor. "How's this?"

"Good," Maddie said. "But why did you put a swing in the house?"

"So you'll have something to do when it rains. The weather won't always be nice." He set the swing in motion. "Try it out."

Maddie sat in the seat and grasped the chains. She pushed off gently. Her toes skimmed the floor. Overhead the chains made a funny sound. *Squee, squee.* Maddie stopped.

"That's just the metal chains on the metal brace," Sam said. "It won't break. How's the seat?"

"Fine." She almost said, "Perfect." This time she

pushed off harder. Her feet swept out as a rush of musty basement air blew her bangs.

"You can listen to my old radio," Sam said. "Or you can read those old storybooks."

"Read on a swing?" Her stomach flipped over at the very idea.

"Not really swinging. Just rocking back and forth."

Maddie remembered the fairy tale book with the old-fashioned pictures. The next rainy day, maybe she'd read a story sitting in the swing. It sounded like fun.

Now she pumped high enough to look out one of the half windows. Her dogwood tree rose into view. The trunk wasn't as stick-like, she noticed. It was getting thicker. And taller.

Maddie breezed back. *Squee-squee!* It had been a pretty good day. She and Sam had gotten into trouble together. They hunted for treasure and been fooled by the dump. She had a reading-swing. Maybe Sam knew more about eight-year-old kids than she thought.

"Guess what the swing's name is?" she asked Sam as she sailed past.

"What?"

"Ruby," said Maddie and pointed her toes to the ceiling.

Buckingham Runs Away

"*G*uess what?" Maddie said to her stuffed donkey. "We're going to Manassas!"

Buckingham sat next to a shoebox overflowing with little dresses, skirts, and blouses. Her ears looked straighter, and her eyes seemed brighter.

Maddie picked out a yellow sundress she had made herself. The stitches were big and crooked, but at least she could make real clothes now. She used to cut a hole in a piece of material. Then her mother taught Maddie to sew a seam.

Abraham watched from the doorway as Maddie put the dress on Buckingham.

"If you weren't such a grumpy old cat, I'd make you a dress," Maddie told him. "No, costumes! We could put on plays!"

Abraham swished away, letting her know what *he* thought of that idea.

"Come on, Maddie," her mother called.

Maddie stuck a pin with a yellow bow into Buckingham's plush head, then ran into the kitchen. Her mother was nervously jingling the keys to Sam's truck. Her car was in the shop.

"What if I shift too slow at red lights and it stalls?" she was saying to Sam.

"You know how to drive stick shift. Have faith." He kissed her cheek. "Just don't forget the seven-foot bed when you park."

"You aren't coming with us?" Maddie asked.

"Got to finish a set of bookcases." With a wink, he added, "Keep an eye on your mother."

Outside, Maddie and Buckingham climbed into Chester's passenger seat.

Her mother turned the key and backed slowly out of the driveway. Sam waved at them.

"Here we go," said Maddie's mother as they pulled onto Lee Highway.

"Off to a Perfect Day!" Maddie chirped. "This is just like the old days—me and you and Buckingham."

"Except I'm driving Sam's truck," her mother said. "When we lived in town, we rode the bus."

"Look, Mrs. Tompkins is in her garden. Hi, Mrs. Tompkins!" Maddie called as they passed. "And there's George's store. Can we stop on the way home?"

"Not today," her mother said. "The carpet man is delivering our new rug this afternoon."

In town, Maddie's mother found a parking space she could pull the truck into. "Now I don't have to worry about that seven-foot bed," she said.

Maddie fed the parking meter three quarters, then cranked the handle. A wheel appeared in the glass window, and the meter began whirring like a very fast clock.

"One hour and fifty-five minutes," said her mother. "That's how much time we have to get everything done."

She took Maddie's hand, and they crossed the street. Maddie held Buckingham in the crook of her elbow. That way, Buckingham could see where they were going.

"Where to first?" Maddie asked, swinging her mother's arm like a jump rope. "The library? The bakery?" The bakery owner, Mrs. Delaney, always gave Maddie a free sugar cookie.

"Maddie, please. I can't read with all this jiggling." Her mother took a list from her purse and glanced at the first item. "The bank."

Inside the bank, Maddie propped Buckingham on the slanty desk. She wrapped the silver chain that held the ballpoint pen around Buckingham's wrist like a bracelet.

A man came over with some papers. "May I borrow your pen, Madame?" he asked Buckingham in a gallant voice.

"She hasn't learned to write anyway," Maddie said. She unwrapped the pen and handed it to the him.

"Come on, Maddie." Her mother signaled that they were leaving.

Next they went to the library, Maddie's favorite place in the world, though George's store ran a close second.

"Choose two books," she told Maddie. "I'm sorry, that's all the time we have today."

Maddie felt a pinch of dismay. On their old Perfect Days, she would take her time picking out books, as many as she wanted. But because of the whirring meter, Maddie chose two chapter books without even looking to see if they had pictures inside.

On the library steps, her mother checked her list again. "The bakery."

Mrs. Delaney wasn't behind the counter of the

Corner Bakery. Instead a girl chewing gum waited on customers. Maddie breathed in the heavenly smell of fresh-baked bread. She wanted to powder her face with the pillowy donuts.

Her mother bought loaves of whole-wheat bread and the sandwich rolls Sam loved. The gum-chewing girl filled bags but did not offer a free cookie to Maddie.

Maddie was disappointed. Her Perfect Day was rapidly becoming not-so-perfect.

"Now where?" she asked her mother.

"Sears. It's two blocks over." Her mother juggled the library books, bakery sacks, and her purse.

"Where's your green shopping bag?" asked Maddie.

"Home. Since we drove the truck, I didn't think we'd need it." Her mother handed Maddie her library books. "Could you carry those, sweetie? My arms are full."

In Sears, they headed to the appliance department. Her mother talked to the clerk about a new part for their dishwasher. Maddie strolled around shiny new appliances. She peered into freezers. Buckingham whirled around on the turntable of a microwave.

Her mother dragged over a large box. "I don't know why one part has to be packaged in such a big box." She hitched the strap of her purse over her shoulder, then picked up the box in both hands. "Maddie, will you put the bread on top?"

Maddie piled the bakery sacks on the box, but the rolls kept slipping off. "I'll carry those," she said, tucking her books under her arm. She carried a bakery sack in each hand. Buckingham was stuffed unceremoniously into one of the sacks.

"We have just enough time for lunch at Rudy's," said her mother, setting off at a brisk pace through the park.

Maddie always ran over to the horse statue and touched the right hind hoof for good luck. But today she had to dash through the park and barely even saw the statue.

"Oh, no," her mother said when they entered Rudy's. "We hit the lunch crowd. All the tables are taken. Only two seats left at the counter."

Maddie preferred sitting at the counter anyway. Underneath was a shelf for packages. That was Buckingham's private dining nook.

Today, though, they needed the shelf for all their belongings. Her mother jammed the Sears box on the floor between their stools.

"Look who's back!" sang a waitress with a blonde ponytail. The curly writing on her pocket said *Trish*. "My favorite customers! How's life in the country?"

"We love it," said Maddie's mother. "We have a huge yard—"

"And a garden," Maddie chimed in, "with flowers *and* corn *and* tomatoes."

"Sounds divine." Trish whipped out her pad. "The usual?"

Maddie nodded. She always ordered a grilled cheese sandwich with shoestring potatoes. Even though she could get cheese sandwiches at home, they were better at Rudy's. And she loved the name *shoestring potatoes*.

Trish soon brought two thick china plates and re-filled their water glasses.

"Do you want my cranberry sauce?" asked Maddie's mother. She always ordered a hot turkey sandwich.

Maddie reached for the tiny pleated paper cup of cranberry sauce. "Thanks."

They ate in silence for a moment. It felt good to sit down and not rush all over town.

"Mom," said Maddie. "What's divine mean?"

"It's another word for wonderful."

"Dee-viiiiiiine." Maddie tasted the word, idly swinging her legs and nibbling her French fries one at a time. Then she tried eating her fries end to end, like a licorice whip.

Her mother glanced at the clock over the milkshake machine. "Finish your sandwich, Maddie. We have to go in a minute."

"Don't we get dessert?" asked Maddie, shocked.

"Sorry, sweetie. We really do have to get home."

Maddie stared at her. "But—we always share a maple

walnut sundae. That's what we *do* on a Perfect Day!"

Her mother patted her arm. "It's still a good day. I'm making strawberry shortcake for supper."

Strawberry shortcake hours away hardly made up for a hot fudge sundae served immediately after grilled cheese and shoestring fries. Tears stung Maddie's eyes. She had waited so long for a Perfect Day in town. And look how it turned out!

"People are waiting to use our seats," her mother said, after paying the bill.

They gathered up bags and books and the box, then squeezed their way out of the jam-packed restaurant.

When they reached the parking lot, Maddie ran ahead to check the meter. "Still whirring!" she reported.

"Four minutes to spare!" Her mother piled the packages in the bed of Sam's truck. "At least we have plenty of room for all our things."

On the way home, Maddie sat by the window. She thought about the things that didn't happen on her

Perfect Day. No free cookie, no time to pick out lots of books, no lucky horse hoof. And no maple sundae.

Soon her mother was pulling into their driveway.

"We made it," her mother said with a relieved sigh. "And not a single scratch on Chester. Sam will be happy. I'll make some iced tea. You and Buckingham and I will sit on the back porch and cool off. How's that?"

At the mention of Buckingham's name, Maddie's knees weakened. Where *was* Buckingham? Maddie felt around the seat. Not there. She leaned over to look on the floor and under the seat. Not there either.

"What's wrong?" her mother asked, opening the door.

"I don't know where Buckingham is!"

"I saw you put her in the bakery bag." Her mother paused. "I think I hear the phone ringing." She hurried into the house.

Maddie clambored up on Chester's running board and tore through every bag. Bread, rolls, and library books were scattered all over the truck bed. She turned the bags inside out. But she could not find Buckingham.

Buckingham was gone.

Sam walked over from his workshop. "I see my truck's still in one piece—"

Maddie burst into tears. "I lost Buckingham!"

"What? Where?"

"I don't know!" she wailed. The thought of Buckingham alone in town, maybe lying face down in a mud puddle, maybe being *stepped* on, made Maddie cry harder.

"Calm down," Sam said gently. "Try to remember what you did with her."

"I put her in the bakery bag. But she's not there now! She's not in any bag!"

Maddie's mother came out. "That was the carpet man. He's on his way." She saw Maddie's tear-streaked face. "Maddie! What happened?"

"She lost Buckingham someplace," Sam answered.

"Oh, Maddie! Are you sure she's not in any of the bags?"

Maddie shook her head miserably. "We have to go back and look for her!"

Her mother glanced at Sam. "I must wait for the carpet man. I said I'd be here. And your customer is waiting for those bookcases."

"Bookcases can wait," Sam said, opening Chester's passenger door. "Missing donkeys can't."

Maddie eagerly climbed in. Sam buckled her in, started Chester, and they were off to town again.

"Where did you see Buckingham last?" asked Sam.

Maddie thought. "I stuck her in one of the bakery bags. After we left Rudy's. No, *before* we went to Sears."

"You're sure you put her in the bag before you went in Sears?"

"Positive."

"Absolutely, positively sure?" he asked.

Maddie tried to picture where she was when she put Buckingham in the bag. She could see Buckingham's yellow bow. And she knew Buckingham was miffed because she couldn't see out of the bag. But Maddie could not remember where they were at the time.

"No! I'm not sure!" She burst into tears all over again.

"It's okay," Sam said. "We'll find her." He tapped the steering wheel as if he'd just figured out something. "You know what I bet happened?"

Maddie sniffed. "What?"

"Buckingham got tired of being crammed in that old bag and ran away."

"Ran away? Why would she do that? She's my friend," she said.

Maddie remembered waiting at the apartment window for her father to come back. She remembered the soft, fuzzy feel of Buckingham on her lap. Buckingham *was* her friend.

"Oh, she didn't run away because she was mad at you," Sam said. "She just wanted to scare you a little."

Maddie considered that possibility. "She *does* like getting her own way. I could tell she didn't like being in that bag."

"When we find her, I'll bet she's sorry," he said. "For making you worry."

"I ought to put her in the time-out corner!" Maddie exclaimed.

In town, Maddie directed Sam to the exact parking space they had used earlier. Luckily no one was in it. They got out and searched the parking lot. No Buckingham.

"We'll retrace your steps," Sam told her. "Where did you go first?"

"The bank. Buckingham played with the pen on a chain and some man needed it."

She took Sam's hand as they crossed the street. She had never done this before. When they were out together, she always held her mother's hand. But today she needed Sam's. His big fingers were rough, but warm. She felt a little better.

The bank teller, who remembered Maddie and her mother, told them he hadn't seen a small stuffed donkey wearing a yellow sundress.

Neither had the librarian. "If someone finds her here, I'll call you at home."

The gum-chewing girl at the Corner Bakery shook her head when Sam asked if she had seen Buckingham. "No one has turned in any stuffed animal."

"Thanks," Sam said, leading Maddie out of the store. "Where to next?"

Maddie had to think. "Sears! Buckingham rode in a microwave."

In the appliance section, she and Sam opened and closed every single microwave, dishwasher, refrigerator, freezer, and oven door. Empty.

When they asked the clerk, he said, "Check Lost and Found in Customer Service."

"She must be there!" Maddie said, pulling Sam through the aisles.

But she wasn't.

Outside Sears, Maddie sobbed, "She's gone forever!

I'll never see her again!"

Sam stooped so his face was level with hers and laid his hands on her shoulders. "Listen to me. Don't give up on Buckingham. She's tired of her joke by now and wants you to come get her. She's afraid."

Maddie was too. Everything in her life had changed, but Buckingham had always been there, looking at Maddie with her bright button eyes.

"Where did you and your mother go next?" asked Sam.

"Rudy's. Oh, Sam! Rudy's was so crowded! Mom and me could hardly get a seat—"

"Are you giving up before we even get there? Have a little faith."

As they walked to the restaurant, Maddie's feet felt like lead. She was trying to have faith, like Sam said. If she only knew what faith *looked* like, the way she knew every worn place in Buckingham's fur, every frayed thread.

She opened Rudy's door with dread. Only a few tables were occupied at this time of day. The waitresses, rushed off their feet a few hours earlier, were leisurely refilling salt and pepper shakers. One man sat at the counter, sipping coffee and chatting with Trish.

Trish saw Maddie and Sam. She winked and pointed with a pink-tipped fingernail.

There, propped against a chrome napkin dispenser, sat Buckingham in her yellow sundress, the yellow bow stuck in her plush head.

"You found her!" Maddie ran to the counter. She grabbed Buckingham and said sternly, "Don't you ever run away again!"

Coffee Man held up his cup in a salute. "You gotta be firm with 'em."

"Thanks so much," Sam said to Trish. "Where was Buckingham?"

"Poor thing was stuck under the counter shelf," Trish said. "If Maddie hadn't come back by this evening, I was going to call." She stuck out her hand. "You must be Sam. Y'all sit down and we'll celebrate. Maple walnut sundaes on the house!"

"Oh, boy!" Maddie wiggled up on a stool. "They make the best maple walnut sundaes in the world here!"

"I like extra whipped cream," Sam said expansively.

"Me too," said Coffee Man.

"Me three!" Maddie said. She thought back to that morning, when the day was fresh and new. "You told me to keep an eye on Mom. I should have kept an eye on Buckingham!"

Trish brought the first sundae and set it in front of Maddie.

"Sam and I will share ours," she said. "If that's okay with Sam."

"First one to dig in gets the cherry," he said with a grin.

Maddie plunged her spoon into the mound of ice cream while Buckingham watched with bright button eyes.

"Dee-vine!" said Maddie.

The Tree House

"Knee high." Sam measured the height of a corn stalk against his leg. "Right on schedule."

"What's on schedule?" Maddie asked. She nibbled a blade of grass. It tasted exactly the way she expected grass to taste. Green, and a little like celery.

"Corn should be knee high by the fourth of July," said Sam. "Then it tassels and then it makes. Pretty soon we'll be eating corn on the cob with butter running down our chin."

Maddie took the grass out of her mouth and studied the teeth marks along the stem. She was more used to Sam now, but she still didn't understand a lot of what he said.

He looked across the cornfield. "Why is there a board in the sweetgum tree?" he asked.

"That's my tree house," said Maddie. "The board was on the floor in the shed. I hope you don't mind I took it."

"No, I don't mind. But how can one little board be a tree house?"

"I'll show you."

They left the corn patch and walked over to where the yard and woods met. Maddie often played there. The trees seemed tamer, not as tall and forbidding as the trees deep in the woods. Yet the yard was wilder, unlike the neat, clipped lawn around the house. Tiny wild strawberries grew close to the ground, among pale blue flowers that trembled on stems finer than hairs.

Maddie had wedged her board in the crotch of a branch so low, she only had to hitch herself up to sit on it.

Sam waggled the board back and forth. "You didn't nail it down."

"It doesn't move much." She demonstrated. "My lunch box goes on this little branch. And Buckingham sits here."

"Hmmm." Sam studied the arrangement. "How would you like a real tree house?"

"Like in that old book?" She'd found a boy's storybook among her reading-swing books. "I don't want to hurt a tree sticking it with a bunch of nails."

After George gave her the idea, she thought it would be neat to live in a tree. But she was so afraid of high places. If she told Sam, he would think she was a baby.

"I think we can do better than this," he said. "You should have a special place of your own."

"I have bedroom of my own," said Maddie.

"In the house," Sam pointed out. "You can fix up

your tree house any way you want."

There was no stopping Sam once he got hold of an idea, Maddie knew. He marched out to the shed and sorted through his pile of lumber. After Sam loaded Chester with lumber, sawhorses, toolbox, and ladder, they drove back to the edge of the woods.

"This tree is perfect." He pushed against an oak as if testing its sturdiness.

Maddie looked at it doubtfully. She liked the friendly canopy of leaves and little bunches of acorns. But the first branch of the tree was at least a mile up!

Sam got busy. He measured and cut boards and laid them in a square. Maddie stood inside the square and tried to imagine a house with walls, floor, and a roof.

"Which branch are you going to use?" she asked, worried. "The big one?"

"Nope."

Now Maddie was really worried. "Not the one *above* the first branch?" The next branch appeared to scrape the sky.

"Not that one either." Sam reeled his tape measure into the steel case. "No branch."

"How can a tree house not be in a branch?"

"You'll see."

All afternoon, Sam hammered and sawed. He stood four posts on end and nailed the square frame to them. Then he clambered up his ladder and began laying planks for the floor.

Maddie watched from the ground, twiddling twigs in little mountains of sawdust.

Sam leaned over the platform. "How would you like to come up?"

"I can't," she said. "I'm—I mean, Buckingham is afraid of ladders."

She hoped Sam wouldn't suggest she toss Buckingham up to him. Then she'd have to admit the truth that *she* was scared.

Sam came back down. "I'll help. Give Miss Bucky to me." He put her inside his shirt. "Now all you have to do is hold on to the rails and take it one rung at a time."

But Maddie could not put even one foot on the bottom rung. She kept thinking about the time she climbed the jungle gym.

"Watch Maddie," her mother had told Maddie's father as they left for the park. But he didn't. He didn't see her pull herself up bar by bar, and then lose her balance.

"I won't let you fall," Sam promised.

She started to raise her right foot to the bottom rung, then stopped. "What if my foot slips?"

"See that rough stuff on the rung?" Sam said. "Those strips keep your feet from skidding."

She took a deep breath, let it out. She did like the idea of having a place all her own. But how could she play in her tree house if she couldn't climb a ladder?

"When you're ready, we'll go up together," said Sam.

Finally Maddie placed her right foot on the bottom rung. Then her left. The ladder quivered a bit. She glanced nervously at Sam.

"That's just the ladder taking your weight," he reassured her. "Nothing to worry about."

Maddie climbed up another rung, and another. Three steps off the ground made a huge difference. She was up so high! Sam stayed right behind her, his big hands holding onto the rails just below hers.

Maddie looked down to see the next step.

"Don't look down," he said. "Keep your eyes straight ahead."

"I have to see where my foot goes!" She gripped the rails so tight her knuckles turned white.

"Do you want to go back down?"

She did, but she hated being a baby even worse.

"No," she said uncertainly. "Just give me a sec."

"Take your time." His voice was calm and low. "Did I ever tell you about my chinquapin bush?"

"Your what?" Maddie's hands unclenched from the rails, and she ventured up another step.

"Chinquapin bush. Chinquapins are the sweetest, tastiest nuts in the world." Behind her, Sam moved up when Maddie did.

"Better than cashews?" She loved cashews and was always delighted whenever Sam brought her a small bag.

"Lots better. And they grow wild. When I was a kid, we had a chinquapin bush along the road near our house. I used to fill my pockets while I waited for the bus and eat them on the way to school. Boy, were they good."

Maddie's mouth watered. A nut that tasted better than cashews and was *free*!

"Can we go to your old house and pick some today?" she asked, crawling up two more rungs.

"I wish we could," he replied. "A long time ago, a disease killed all the chestnut trees. That same disease killed most of the chinquapin bushes, too. The bush near my old house died years ago."

"So there aren't any more chinka-things?" She climbed two more steps. The platform of her tree house was eye level. She clutched the rails again.

"This part isn't as hard as it seems," Sam said softly. "Climb up one more rung, and I'll lift you the rest of the way."

Maddie froze. Sam was wrong. This part *was* hard. The ground was so far down! She wanted to be on it more than anything in the world.

"Climb one more step, and I'll tell you about my secret bush, maybe the last chinquapin bush."

"Is it in our woods?" Maddie guessed, inching her hands up the rails. Her foot felt heavy, but she brought it up to the last rung.

Sam moved up, too, then plucked her off the ladder and set her on the platform.

Maddie sat down with a plunk. Tears pricked her eyes. It was too much, all this height, all at once. She felt safer sitting down.

Sam pulled Buckingham from his pocket and sat down, too. "You did it, Miss Bucky. See? It wasn't so bad."

"I did it, too, didn't I?" Maddie let out a long *whoosh* of a breath. Had she been holding it the whole time?

"I did, didn't I?" she said in wonder. "Okay, tell me about the last chinquapin bush." Now that she was on the platform, she relaxed.

"You were right—it is in our woods."

"How come that bush didn't get the disease and die?"

"I think because it's growing by itself," Sam said. "The disease spread from chestnut tree to chestnut tree and from chinquapin bush to chinquapin bush. But there are only oak trees around this one little old bush."

"Can we go get some of those nuts?" she asked.

"They won't be ripe till later this summer," Sam told her. "We'll go then." He headed toward the ladder. "I'm going down for more lumber. Sit back and watch your tree house grow around you."

The rest of the afternoon, Sam built three walls with windows. The fourth wall had a doorway and a window. A slanted roof stuck out over the windows on the doorway wall so rain wouldn't drip in.

But the most amazing thing about Maddie's tree house was that it was not in the tree! The whole structure perched on four stilts. The house was attached to the tree trunk with wood braces.

"We're not hurting the tree at all," said Sam. "This old oak will like having company besides birds and squirrels."

Maddie looked out each window. In her little house tucked under the leafy umbrella, she felt like a squirrel herself. Or a bird in a nest. Now she could be part of the margin between woods and yard, wild and ordinary.

Then an uneasy feeling crept over her. How was she going to get *down*? The tree house in that old boy's book had a knotted rope for a ladder. She couldn't shimmy up and down a dangling rope in a million years.

Would Sam leave his metal ladder with the no-slip steps? But that wouldn't help. She was more afraid of climbing down ladders than going up.

"How am I going to get up and down?" she asked fearfully.

"You'll see." His famous words.

On the ground, Sam hammered smaller boards inside two wide, notched boards. Maddie lay on her stomach and peered through the doorway. When he raised the boards, she saw a staircase, just like in a real house.

Sam firmly nailed the staircase just below the doorway. "Be right back."

After he left, Maddie gingerly tested the first step, then quickly pulled her foot back. The staircase was great, but there was nothing to hang onto.

She sat down in the doorway again and thought about how she would decorate her private place. Her mother had a pink plastic shower curtain left over from their apartment. Maddie could cut it up and hang the pieces at her windows. Maybe her mother would let her have the old pink bath mat that went with it.

But what was the point in making plans when she was too afraid to climb up and down the stairs?

Abraham strolled out of the woods from one of his mysterious cat missions. He looked up at the tree house where Maddie sat slumped in the doorway.

Then he walked up the staircase with sure-footed purpose.

Maddie admired his bravery. Abraham was no chicken. Mrs. Thomkin's *chickens* weren't as chicken as she was.

"Stay up here with me," Maddie said to the cat, squeezing him in a hug.

But he oozed out of her grasp and trotted back down the stairs with an indignant flick of his tail. Maddie sighed. Abraham was still very much Sam's cat.

Sam came back carrying two long poles. They looked like the poles he'd made to prop up the clothesline, only longer.

"Almost done." He nailed the poles on either side of the staircase.

Maddie grinned. Handrails! That Sam was so smart! Nobody in the world had a not-in-a-tree tree house with a real staircase and handrails.

Sam stood at the bottom and looked up encouragingly. "Try it out!"

Using the handrails, Maddie walked down the stairs. He had set the steps close together, so she didn't feel the least bit wobbly. Then she walked up the stairs.

"It works!" she said, coming back down again. "You're a good builder!"

"Glad you like it. Now you have your own special place."

As they drove Chester back to the shed with the tools and scrap lumber, Sam said, "You were very brave climbing that ladder."

"I was?" she said. "I felt like a big chicken. I don't like being afraid of things. But I am."

"Everybody is afraid of something."

She looked over at him. "Even you?"

"Even me."

Maddie couldn't imagine what Sam would ever be afraid of. He could do anything.

He had spent all day building her a tree house. A special tree house, made just for her. She wished she could give him something, too.

She thought a moment and said, "If you get scared, you can talk to me about it."

Sam stopped Chester in front of the shed door. He gave her a broad smile. "That's the nicest thing anybody's said to me in a long time."

Maddie got out of the truck, feeling good inside. She didn't know whether it was because of her new tree house or because she'd made Sam smile.

Abraham had followed them to the shed. He twined around Maddie's legs, his tail arched like a question mark.

"You never come when I call, but now you want to be nice," she said. "Race you back to the house!"

She sprinted across the yard. Abraham streaked past and was waiting for her on the porch. He yawned, showing it had been an easy victory.

"Just for this you can't come in my new tree house!" Maddie flung herself down beside him. "Okay, you can. But you have to learn the password."

He washed his left paw.

"The *password*," she said, "is *Abraham.*" That'd get him!

Abraham looked at her with half-closed eyes, as if to say, *You'll see*.

The Last Chinquapin Bush

"Will we see snakes?" Maddie asked.

The August sun glared down as they crossed the back yard. It made the white sky look stretched and tight, like the underside of a circus tent.

"Maybe, but probably not," Sam replied. "Heat makes 'em kind of sluggish."

Maddie didn't care about snakes today anyway. Well, not too much. She was still afraid of the deep woods beyond her tree house. The strange dark trees, the whispers and rustlings of wild animals.

But today she and Sam were going to find Sam's famous chinquapin bush!

All week she had wondered about the chinquapin bush. What did it look like? She pictured red and green and yellow chinquapins hanging from the branches like ornaments on a Christmas tree.

Now her mouth watered at the thought of tasting her first chinquapin. Sam had said they were better than any nut in the world, even better than cashews.

"How will we find one bush in all these woods?" she asked.

"It's near an old rail fence. If it's still there."

Maddie swung her lunch box. "I'm going to fill this with chinquapins. Some for you and some for Mom, but most for me! Maybe *one* for Abraham."

She glanced at the cat, who was staring intently at a ridge that rippled the lawn like a small mountain range. Abraham still wouldn't come to her, no matter how sweetly she called his name. He wouldn't even come when she offered him a treat.

"I don't think Abraham is much of a nut eater," Sam said. "Right now he's waiting for that mole to move."

He crashed a path through heavy brush with his thick-soled boots. Maddie ducked under low-hanging branches he held back for her. Blackberry whips snagged her long sleeves, and burrs hitchhiked on her socks.

"It's like a jungle in here," she said, breathing hard.

"Once we're past the undergrowth, it gets easier," said Sam.

Halfway up a steep hill, Maddie tripped over a root. A flash of blue flew past with a laughing cry.

"What's so funny?" Maddie yelled at the bird.

Sam helped her up. A smile twitched at the corners of his mouth.

"Don't you laugh too!" she said indignantly. "It's bad enough that bird did."

"Blue jays laugh at everybody," Sam told her.

The Last Chinquapin Bush

They kept walking, slogging through years and years of fallen leaves. It was like wading through crinkly brown snowdrifts.

Oaks and poplars and pines loomed over them like ancient kings and queens. Maddie sensed royalty in the straightness of their proud trunks, the crowns of green leaves they wore. She felt small and unimportant and was glad Sam led the way. She wasn't sure the trees would let her pass, just her alone.

When they reached the top of the hill, she groaned. "Not *another* hill. All we do is walk up and down hills. Where is the chinquapin bush?"

"We're almost there. Want to rest?"

"No." She didn't want Sam to think she wasn't as tough as he was.

They tackled the second slope, steeper than the first. Maddie thought the woods would be a quiet place. But she and Sam made a terrific racket, kicking shin-high piles of leaves and cracking fallen sticks. At the bottom of the hill, the land leveled and the trees weren't so dense.

"There's the fence," said Sam.

Maddie looked but didn't see anything. "What fence?"

"Here." He walked over to a couple of skinny gray saplings lying on the ground.

Maddie noticed the saplings had been shaped by tools, like the poles Sam had cut for their bean vines to climb.

"Fences are supposed to be made of boards," she said.

"This is a split-rail fence," Sam said. "Built without nails. In the old days, people learned to make do without things we take for granted, like nails."

"It's on the ground," she said critically. "Shouldn't it be standing up?"

Sam knelt and stroked the deep weathered grooves. "This fence dates back to the Civil War, Maddie."

"When was that?"

"A long, long time ago. Before either of us was born."

Even if the fence was really old, it wasn't very interesting. She looked around. "Where's the chinquapin bush? You said it was here."

Sam stood up. "It is. Just past that big poplar."

Maddie's eyes followed the twin trunks of the poplar tree up and up. They seemed to disappear into the sky like the towers of a wizard's castle. Then she ran ahead of Sam. She wanted to be the first to find the chinquapin bush, the first to pick one of those amazing nuts.

Behind her, Sam stopped.

Maddie stopped too and ran back. "Where's the bush? I don't see it."

None of the bushes around them had brightly colored nuts hanging like Christmas ornaments.

He sighed. "I was afraid of that."

"What? What were you afraid of?" Maddie hopped from foot to foot, flapping her hands.

"The bush is gone, Maddie. It must have died."

"Why would a bush *die*? Don't they grow forever?"

"Remember?" he said. "The disease that killed all chestnut trees and the chinquapin bushes?"

"But *your* bush lived," she insisted. "You used to come here and pick chinquapins."

Sam gently tugged a piece of her hair. "Sorry, kiddo. I haven't been here in a few years. The bush must have died since then, the way the old fence fell down."

Tears welled in Maddie's eyes. It was stupid to cry over a dumb bush, but Sam's bush was the last one in the entire world. She had waited so long to taste the best nuts ever. And now she never would. It didn't seem fair, somehow.

"Are you okay?" Sam asked.

Maddie blinked back the tears so Sam wouldn't think she was a crybaby.

"I'm fine." Though she wasn't, really. "Are we going back now?"

"Not yet. There's one more thing you might like to see. Can you climb one more hill?"

"Okay," she said without enthusiasm. This time she wouldn't get her hopes up.

At the top of the hill, Sam hesitated. "Do you hear it?"

"Hear what?"

"Shhh. Just listen."

She did, but still couldn't hear anything. "What's down there?"

"You'll see."

For once, Maddie didn't feel excited when he said those words. She walked stilt-legged down the other side of the hill, way ahead of Sam. Her hair clung to her neck. She was hot and tired.

At the bottom the land slanted downward. The trees were greener and grew in a wavy line, as if following a path. Maddie heard a soft, bubbling sound.

"Water!" she cried. "That's *water*!"

Shrieking with delight, she dashed to the edge of a tiny, crooked stream and flung herself stomach down on the mossy bank. The air felt cool on her sweaty face.

"What do you think of Willow Spring?" Sam sat down on a rotted log and mopped his red face with a bandanna.

"It's beautiful!" Maddie leaned over and dipped her fingers into the silky water.

The creek wasn't very wide, but it had carved a deep channel. Beneath the bank, a sandbar jutted out like a doll-sized beach.

"Can we go down there?" she asked.

"Sure." Sam jumped down, then helped Maddie scramble down the bank. "Look." He pointed to a line of tracks stamped in the yellow mud.

Maddie squatted and touched one of the footprints. "What kind of animal made those?"

"Raccoon. They are very clean animals—they wash their food before they eat. See their long fingers? Their paws are like little hands."

Maddie was totally entranced by the creek. She loved the delicious coolness of the air and the sound of water rushing over moss-slicked stones. Water really *did* burble, just like stories said it did! The creek was a magical kingdom where anything could happen.

"Is it ours?" she asked Sam.

"The creek? Well, it does go through our property," he replied. "Technically, I suppose that section belongs to us. But I don't think a creek is something you can own. How can you own water and rocks and mud and minnows? A creek belongs to itself."

Maddie trailed her hand in the greenish water. A leaf floated downstream and brushed against her fingers. Then it swirled giddily around the bend.

"Where do you think that leaf is going?" she asked.

"Well, Willow Spring runs east to west, instead of west to east like most streams," Sam said. "It dumps into Cub Run near Manassas, and Cub Run dumps into the Bull Run River. Then I guess it goes to the Potomac River and down into the Chesapeake Bay. The last stop is the Atlantic Ocean."

Maddie marveled over the leaf's long, thrilling journey. She had seen the ocean once, years ago with her parents. Her father had been annoyed because Maddie wouldn't follow him into the tumbling waves.

He called for her to splash over to him, but she kept walking backward, away from the water.

"How long will it take that leaf to get to the ocean?" she asked Sam.

"Maybe a month. That's if the leaf doesn't get hung up on a tree branch or a rock or something." He opened his pocketknife and swiped the blade back and forth on the sole of his boot.

Next Maddie discovered tiny flowers growing in the moss. "Look at these teensy flowers, Sam! Aren't they cute? They look like stars."

"Mmmm." He was bent down, busy prying up something with the blade of his knife, and didn't look up.

Maddie walked along the sandbank in the direction of her leaf. What else would she find? Maybe a talking frog wearing a gold crown! The thought made her giggle.

The creek curved around fallen trees. Chunks of the bank sometimes crumbled into the water, splitting the creek into two streams. Maddie was led farther and farther by the murmuring water, by the promise of another delight around the next bend. She picked up smooth white stones and, once, a bright blue feather.

When she started to put these treasures in her lunch box, she realized with a start that her lunch box was back with Sam. And Sam was . . . where *was* he? How far had she wandered downstream?

"Sam?" Maddie looked back. She didn't see him, or the sandbar, or the mossy bank. She didn't recognize anything around her. The trees seemed closer together.

She turned and began running back upstream. Brambles clawed at her pants, and twigs raked her hair. The woods were after her! She ran faster.

"Sam!" she yelled. "Sam! Where are you?"

Her voice came back at her like the cry of the laughing blue jay. *Sam!* it mocked. *Where are you?*

She hurried around the curves that had lured her on, dragging herself over fallen logs. The white stones dropped from her fingers. The feather fluttered to the ground.

Oh, she'd done it now. Sam would be furious. He'd tell her mother, *Do you know what Maddie did? She ran off in the woods like a two-year-old!*

What if Sam mad was enough to make them leave? Or worse, make her leave. Where would she go?

She stumbled along the creek. Her breath caught in her throat. The air wasn't so refreshing anymore. Her face was sticky from running.

"Maddie? Maddie, yell so I can hear you!"

Sam!

"Sam!" Maddie yelled with all her might.

Sam burst through the trees. "Thank heaven you're okay!" He scooped her up in a bear hug. "Don't ever do that again! You scared me half to death! I was so afraid you'd fallen in the creek!"

Maddie buried her face in his shirt. "I didn't mean to go off! I just wanted to be alone with the creek."

He held her away. "You're mad at me because the chinquapin bush wasn't there. That's why you ran off, isn't it?"

"No, I was just—" But maybe she *was* a little mad, now that she thought about it.

Sam had given her so many things—the tree house, the swing in the basement, wheelbarrow rides, her very own dogwood tree. She was used to being surprised by his *You'll see*'s. This time she was let down when he failed to produce the chinquapin bush.

"Maddie, I'm sorry the chinquapin bush is gone, but that's no reason to go off by yourself. What if you fell in the creek? What if you got hurt? What would I tell your mother?"

Maddie had a flash of her father's disappointed face as he stood knee-deep in the ocean. Maddie wanted to please him, but she was more afraid of the water.

"I'm sorry." The words came out in a whisper.

She *was* sorry. She never wanted to do anything to upset Sam. He was always doing nice things for her. Even when they couldn't find the chinquapin bush, he showed her the creek to make up for it.

He patted her shoulder. "I know you're sorry. We'd

better head back. You're mother will worry if we're late for lunch."

"I have to get my lunch box."

"It's under that tree."

Maddie picked up her lunch box. "I found some pretty rocks and a feather, but I lost them," she said sadly.

"Look inside," said Sam.

She opened her lunch box. Nestled in a bed of star-flowered moss, was a square of mud. Stamped in the center of the mud was a perfect raccoon track.

"Ooh! I'm afraid to touch it!"

Sam grinned. "I'll make a plaster of Paris cast of it. When the plaster hardens, you'll have the raccoon track forever."

Maddie felt like crying. That was what Sam had been doing when she wandered off down the creek—digging up a raccoon footprint so she could have it.

"Come on," he said cheerfully. "We've got hills to climb before we eat, and I'm starving!"

Together they climbed back up the hill. A breeze tossed the lofty treetops. Maddie thought it was like being in church when the organ played and the music floated to the vaulted ceiling. Why did she think the woods were scary?

"When can we come back to the creek?" she asked.

"Soon," Sam said. "Next time we'll bring your mother."

Maddie's happy feeling swept away like the leaf that brushed her fingers. What if Sam told her mother she had run off? Her mother may not let her go back to the creek, ever.

All the way back to the house, Maddie worried that Sam would tell.

At home, Maddie and her mother and Sam ate lunch and admired the sleek mole Abraham had caught and went to George's store for ice cream.

Never once did Sam mention what had happened at the creek that day.

Sam's Perfect Day

Maddie lay in bed and listened. Birdsong, that's what was missing. And the locusts that had shrilled *cree-cree-cree* high in the trees in July, had slowed to a poky *creee-creee*.

Though it was still hot, summer was winding down. Soon it would be September, and she would go to a new elementary school. But Maddie had a more important worry.

Today was Sam's birthday. She had earned three dollars pulling weeds in the strawberry patch. She needed to buy the exact right present for Sam.

"Maddie, come and eat," her mother called. "I have to go to the store this morning."

Maddie skipped out to the kitchen in her pajamas. This was her last chance!

"Where's Sam?" she asked, sliding into her place. She didn't hear hammering from his workshop.

"He left early to deliver the entertainment center." Her mother set a bowl of Cream of Wheat in front of Maddie.

"I *have* to buy Sam a present today." She tasted her Cream of Wheat. Sweet and soup-thin, just the way she liked it. Beside her chair, Abraham looked up expectantly.

"Make him a card. He loves your drawings."

"I did," said Maddie. "But a card is a puny present to open at a party. Not like that big saw you got him."

"We're not really having a party. Mrs. Tompkins is

coming over after supper for cake and ice cream. Sam will open his presents at lunch."

Maddie dribbled cereal off her spoon onto the floor for Abraham. The cat sniffed, then stalked away, insulted.

"Maddie, I just washed the floor." Her mother wiped up the spill. "Mrs. Tompkins asked me to pick up donuts at the store for her. Finish eating, sweetie. We have a lot to do today."

Her mother drove to the grocery store. They bought Mrs. Tompkins' donuts and the ingredients for Sam's cake. Then her mother drove back toward their house.

"Aren't we going to the mall?" Maddie asked, twisting around in her seat. The mall was in the other direction. "I have to buy something for Sam."

"Sweetie, the mall is fifteen miles away. We were just there on Monday," her mother reminded her. "And last weekend."

Maddie had looked both times, but didn't see anything good enough. Sam deserved something really,

really special.

"Mom!" Maddie begged. "It's for *Sam*."

With a sigh, her mother said, "We'll stop at George's. Okay?"

George was stocking the ice cream freezer when they walked in. "Just got a new kind of Dixie cup. Chocolate, vanilla, with a stripe of strawberry in the middle."

"No, thanks," Maddie said importantly. "I'm here to buy a present for Sam."

"Oh, you'll find lots of stuff." George waved a hand. "Nose around."

Maddie walked up and down each aisle. She picked up a compass. Too much money. Sam knew directions, anyway. Hiking boots were nice, but she could only afford the leather laces.

"There's nothing good," she told her mother, disappointed.

"Look at this nice pocket watch," her mother said. "It's only two-fifty."

"Watches are boring." Maddie fingered the dollar bills in her shorts pocket. Three dollars wouldn't even buy Sam a new hammer. "Can't we go to another store?"

"We have to swing by Mrs. Tompkins', remember? By the time we get home, it'll be lunchtime, and Sam will be back." Her mother held out the watch box. "Are you sure you don't want to get him this?"

"No."

Maddie climbed into the car and laid her head wearily against the seat. She would be the only one giving Sam a crummy old card.

"You know, the saw is from both of us," her mother said. "He'll be thrilled with it."

"I want to give Sam a present just from *me*, that I picked out by myself."

"Sam doesn't need a lot fancy presents," her mother said, pulling into Mrs. Tompkins' driveway.

Mrs. Tompkins rushed out to their car, her chickens clucking around her feet.

"Thank heavens you're here," she said. "These chickens are driving me crazy. I forgot their donuts!"

"Your chickens eat donuts?" Maddie asked, handing her the bag.

"Only as a treat." Mrs. Tompkins crumbled an old-fashioned on the ground. Three of the chickens attacked the crumbs, but the fourth stood apart. "Sadie and Lula and Maisie love plain donuts, but Gert's dainty beak only touches raspberry jelly. Keep your feathers on, Gert. I'm hurrying fast as I can."

"Your chickens are so smart," said Maddie. "Abraham is smart, too, but he still won't come to me. I don't think he'll ever like me."

"He just needs time," said Mrs. Tompkins. "Cats are particular critters. Can you all come inside for a minute?"

Maddie's mother shook her head. "Not today, thanks. I have to bake Sam's cake and fix his lunch. He hasn't opened his presents yet."

One present, Maddie thought glumly.

"Can you wait a sec? I have something for Maddie."
Mrs. Tompkins returned a few moments later with an
old cardboard box. "I found these the other day and
thought you'd like them, Maddie. They were mine
when I was your age."

Maddie peered into the box. Inside was a set of
miniature metal pans and rosebud-painted china
dishes. Real china, not plastic.

Mrs. Tompkins said, a bit nervously, "I hope these
aren't too old-fashioned for you. I really don't know
what kids like these days."

"Oh, no! I love them!" Maddie angled the box toward her mother. "Mom, look! Pans and pancake
turners and silverware and—real china dishes!
Thanks, Mrs. Tompkins!"

Maddie's mother inspected a tiny skillet. "Copper
bottoms! These pans are as good as the ones I use at
home."

"There's even a set of cake tins so you can bake an
itty-bitty layer cake," said Mrs. Tompkins. "The perfect

size for you and Buckingham."

"We've got to go," said Maddie's mother. "See you this evening."

Maddie balanced the box on her knees the short distance home. The cake tin mirrored her face in miniature perfection. Suddenly she knew *exactly* what to give Sam for his birthday.

At home, Maddie's mother mixed the ingredients for Sam's cake. Maddie washed and dried her new pans and dishes and utensils.

"Just enough left over for two tiny layers." Her mother scraped chocolate cake batter into Maddie's cake tins, then slid all the pans into the oven. "We'll have to watch yours so it doesn't burn."

By the time they whipped up the frosting, Maddie's cake was ready to come out. Maddie centered it on the little rosebud platter and swirled on frosting.

The back door thumped. Maddie quickly hid her little cake under a teacup.

"Happy birthday!" she yelled when Sam came in.

He hung his red cap on its peg. "Don't tell me I'm another year older. How did that happen?"

"The calendar did it," said Maddie.

"Let's get rid of the calendar, then. I don't like getting older."

"I do!" Maddie cried. "When I'm nine . . . I'll be divine!"

"You're divine now," Sam said.

Maddie's mother kissed Sam's cheek. "Lunch first or your presents?"

"Well, I'm pretty hungry—"

"Sa-am!" Maddie said. Why would anybody rather *eat* than open presents?

"Okay," he said. "Bring on my birthday loot."

Maddie's mother shot her a twinkly glance. "I'm afraid we can't bring you this present. It's in the garage."

"Is it a new sports car?" he asked.

"Better," said Maddie.

They all trooped out to the garage, even Abraham.

An object squatted in the corner, swathed in a sheet. Maddie jerked off the sheet with a dramatic "Ta-da!" The electric saw stood revealed in all its shiny glory.

"The bandsaw!" Sam ran his hands over the clean metal edges. "How did you know I wanted this?"

"You bent the corner on the page in the tool catalog," said Maddie.

"It was delivered yesterday," said Maddie's mother. "But you never saw it."

"Glad my hints did the trick. Seriously, this is a wonderful present. Thanks." He kissed them both, then said, "*Now* let's eat."

After lunch, Maddie told Sam, "You still have another present. From me."

Sam peeked under his napkin. "I don't see anything. Where is it?"

"It's a surprise. You and Buckingham go out on the porch." Maddie shooed him out the door as if he were one of Mrs. Tompkins' chickens.

With a fruit knife, she cut three tiny triangles from

her frosted cake and flipped the slices onto the three rosebud saucers. She placed the saucers on the matching tray and added three tiny silver forks. Perfect!

Her mother began filling the sink with soapy water. "For heaven's sake, Maddie. Those pieces are no bigger than a mosquito bite. Give him the whole cake."

"Mom, nobody eats a whole cake!" Maddie backed through the screened door, plates jittering on the china tray.

Sam held Buckingham on his knee. His eyebrows lifted when Maddie handed him one of the little plates.

"What's this?"

"Birthday cake!" she said. "I baked it myself! Mrs. Tompkins gave me pans and dishes she had when she was my age."

"Well, well." Sam grasped the tiny fork in his big fingers, but it slipped and clattered to the porch floor.

"Take Buckingham's," Maddie said. But Sam

dropped that one, too. "Just use your fingers."

Sam polished his cake off in one bite. "Delicious! My compliments to the chef!"

"Want to split Buckingham's?" said Maddie.

Sam patted his stomach. "You go ahead. I'm full. Thanks for a great birthday present."

"That's not all." Maddie licked the crumbs from Buckingham's plate.

"There's more?"

"Lots more." She took Sam's hand. "Come on."

They went inside and down the basement stairs. Maddie's lunch box sat at the bottom. Opening it, she gave Sam four sticks of chalk in different colors.

"What do I do with these?" he said.

"See? I erased this part of the wall," she told him. "For you to draw on."

"The only thing I can draw is flies."

Maddie selected a piece of green chalk. "Anybody can draw. It's like—going up a ladder. Just put the chalk on the wall and make a mark. Then make another one."

She wrote "Happy Birthday" in huge letters, then glanced over at Sam's side of the wall. "What are all those checkmarks?"

"Flies."

Maddie pinched back a laugh. She didn't want to hurt Sam's feelings. Maybe he really was a terrible drawer. Then she saw his grin. He was teasing!

They both laughed. Then Sam started back up the stairs.

"Wait! You have more birthday present." Maddie pulled him over to her reading-swing. "Sit in Ruby and I'll read you my favorite story."

But when Sam sat down, the chains bit into his arms and his long legs stuck way out in front of him.

"You don't fit!" It never occurred to Maddie that Sam might be too big for her swing.

"Yes, I do," he insisted. "Let me hear your favorite story."

Maddie turned the yellowed pages of the *Grimm's*

Fairy Tales to "Little One-Eyes, Two-Eyes, and Three-Eyes" and began reading aloud.

"That was a good story," said Sam when she had finished. "Don't you wish you had a magic tree with silver leaves and golden apples?"

"Yeah," Maddie agreed. Then she shook her head. "No, not really. I like our plain old trees just fine. Want the rest of your birthday present?"

"You're really spoiling me." He stood. The swing seat stuck to his rear end. "I may have to wear this the rest of my life."

Maddie giggled as she helped him yank the seat off. Then she led him outside to her tree house. She climbed up first.

"Come on." She made room for him. Sam squeezed through the doorway.

Maddie patted the pink bath mat. "Sit here. You're company."

He folded his legs and sat on the small rug. "You've fixed it up real nice, Maddie. I like the curtains.

Where'd you get that box?"

"At the dump last Sunday." She lifted the lid, revealing gifts from the oak tree. "Look how shiny these acorns are. I'm going to make a bracelet. Will you drill the holes?"

"Sure." Sam tried to stretch his long legs. Maddie realized he didn't fit in her tree house, either. Her shoulders sagged.

"What's wrong?" he said.

"I wanted to give you a Perfect Day for your birthday," she said sadly. "But I gave you *my* Perfect Day. Stuff I like to do. You'd probably rather do grown-up stuff."

"That's not true. This *is* a Perfect Day." He paused. "Remember once when you asked if I was ever afraid of anything?"

She nodded.

"Well, I was really afraid you wouldn't like it here after living in town."

"Really? I love it here!"

She *did*. She loved the woods and the garden. She loved the way the sky seemed bigger and was sometimes tinted a magic pink. She loved the birds that woke her in the morning. She loved feeling she was *in* the world. She belonged here, the way the mockingbird and the oak tree and even the snakes belonged.

"This is the best place," she said firmly.

Sam gazed out the doorway of the tree house. "I got the best present long before my birthday."

"What?"

"You and your mother. All of our days together are perfect."

"Even the day you quit work to look for Buckingham?" she asked. "And the day I got lost in the woods?"

"Okay, not all days are perfect," said Sam. "And that's a good thing. If we had nothing but perfect days, we'd get bored. Having ordinary days and even bad days once in a while makes a Perfect Day really special."

"Even rotten days are okay," Maddie agreed. "Because

we are a family. Mom, me, you. Even Abraham, though he doesn't act like it most of the time."

She looked out the doorway of her tree house, too, and noticed her dogwood tree standing sturdily against the blue sky. The leaves at the top were turning scarlet, as if the tree wore a ruby crown.

Sam's cat lolled in the soft grass under the dogwood, his eyes half closed in that blissful state only cats can reach.

Maddie leaned out the doorway.

"Abraham!" she called.

The cat's eyes flew open.

"Come here!"

He blinked as if he couldn't believe his ears. Maddie could practically read his mind. The little female human giving him an order?

"Abraham!"

Slowly he got to his feet and yawned. Then he padded deliberately across the lawn toward the tree house, as if it was his idea all along to go to Maddie.

Acknowledgements

Some books strike like a bolt of lightning—a fiery flash of an idea that sends me flying to my computer, my notebook, a dry cleaning receipt, any surface on which to capture fleeting thoughts. And some books, like this one, pad in on little cat's feet.

This story crept into my head on a soft spring day when the breeze was filled with maple wings and pear blossoms. I knew the natural world would figure largely, along with lunch boxes and stuffed donkeys, butterscotch pie and ice cream sundaes, county dumps and basement swings, and other important matters under the wide, blue sky.

Snippets of memories tugged at me, some as reluctant as a cat accepting a new owner. When I began to write, I felt as if my clumsy fingers on the keyboard would shatter this fragile thing. To bring this book into being, others came to my rescue.

Marion Dane Bauer, my advisor in the Writing for Children Program at Vermont College, where the book was born, helped cobble the shapeless plot into a structure as sturdy as Sam's tree house.

My agent, Tracey Adams, stood behind this book all the way.

A wheelbarrow heaped with gratitude goes to my editor, Shannon Barefield, who gave Maddie her final, freeing push out into the world.

Thanks as always to my husband, Frank, who believes making books ranks higher than cooking.

Lastly, a special thank you goes to the real Sam, who gave me weeks, months, and years of Perfect Days. I never realized the worth of the man or those ordinary-seeming days until both were gone.

About the Author

Candice Ransom has written more than one hundred books for children, including *Finding Day's Bottom*, which *Booklist* called "an involving story of loss, pain, healing, and family love." Ms. Ransom holds a Master of Fine Arts in writing for children and young adults from Vermont College. She lives in Fredericksburg, Virginia.